D0466896

ROAD TRIP with MAX and His MOM

LINDA URBAN

ILLUSTRATED BY

KATIE KATH

HOUGHTON
MIFFLIN
HARCOURT

Boston New York

Text copyright © 2018 by Linda Urban
Illustrations copyright © 2018 by Katie Kath

All rights reserved.
For information about permission to reproduce selections
from this book, write to trade.permissions@hmhco.com or to
Permissions, Houghton Mifflin Harcourt Publishing Company,
3 Park Avenue, 19th Floor, New York, New York 10016.

hmhco.com

The text was set in 14 pt. Chaparral Pro.
Design by Christine Kettner & Andrea Miller

Library of Congress Cataloging-in-Publication Data is available.

ISBN 978-0-544-80912-3

Printed in the United States of America
DOC 10 9 8 7 6 5 4 3 2 1
4500702377

For Jeannette

The
Announcement

On Monday morning after breakfast, Mom made an announcement. "We are going on an adventure."

Max was surprised. Mom was not the sort of mom who made announcements about adventures. She was the sort of mom who made announcements about the laundry needing to be put away, or how proud she was of Max's report card, or that Max's hair was getting long and it was time for a trim.

"An adventure to the barbershop?" asked Max.

"A real adventure." Mom handed Max a card that said:

BIRTHDAY PARTY AND FAMILY REUNION

Beneath the words was a photo of a very, very old woman wearing a very, very old cowboy hat.

"Your Great-Great-Aunt Victory is turning one hundred years old."

Max was surprised at this, too. "I have a Great-Great-Aunt Victory?"

"You've met her be-fore," said Mom. "When you were three."

Max looked closely at the photo. He did not

remember meeting any very, very old women in cowboy hats.

"You sat in her lap and sang the alphabet song into a soup spoon. It was adorable." Mom said "adorable" in a way that made Max feel like he was still only three years old instead of nine. "My uncles called you Spooner after that. You really don't remember?"

Max was glad he did not remember. Who wanted to remember being called Spooner?

Mom tapped the invitation. "Read the inside," she said.

VICTORY IS TURNING 100
Join us at her favorite spot
in the world,
Bronco Burt's Wild Ride
Amusement Park,
for a day of ropin', ridin',
and reminiscin'!

"Have I been to Bronco Burt's before too?" asked Max.

"No," said Mom. "But I went dozens of times when I was growing up in Pennsylvania."

Max had seen Pennsylvania on the map in Mrs. Maloof's classroom. It didn't even touch Michigan. There was a whole Ohio between. "Pennsylvania is pretty far away."

"That is the best part," said Mom. "You and I are going on a road trip!"

Wow! A birthday party, an amusement park, and a road trip? This *did* sound like an adventure! "Will I get to miss school?" asked Max.

"The party is on Saturday. We'll drive to Pennsylvania after school on Friday and come back on Sunday night. You won't miss a thing," said Mom.

"Oh," said Max.

Mom laughed. "You look disappointed. Guess you really wanted to miss some school, huh?"

Max shook his head. He wouldn't have

minded missing a little school, but that was not why he was disappointed. "I'd like to go with you, but I can't."

"You can't?" asked Mom. "Why not?"

Max got quieter. He did not want Mom to feel bad about her mistake, especially when she sounded so happy. "You work at Shady Acres on the weekends and I go to Dad's, remember?" The schedule was right there on the family calendar, in Mom's no-budge, no-smudge ink. "You only get me on the weekdays."

"That's usually true. But your Great-Great-Aunt Victory will turn one hundred only once. I've talked to your dad and he said if you want to go to the party, you should go. You do want to go, don't you?"

Max did want to go, but he wished he didn't have to leave Dad alone on the weekend. Ever since Dad had gotten his apartment, he and Max had spent the weekends together. They ate pizza and watched movies and walked Ms. Tibbet's basset hounds and had breakfast at Ace's Coffee Shop every morning. What would Dad do without Max to keep him company?

"Oh, Max, you're going to love it," Mom continued. "Bronco Burt's has rides and barbecue stands and a Wild West arcade and . . ." Her face turned dreamy, like it did when she took a bite of her favorite Mocha Monkey Ice Cream. ". . . the Big Buckaroo."

The Big Buckaroo? Who was the Big Buckaroo?

He sounded to Max like some kind of movie-star guy. Since when did Mom care about movie-star guys?

"I have to get to the bus stop," said Max.

Mom looked at the clock. "We still have a few minutes. Don't you want to talk more about our trip?"

"I don't want to be late." Max grabbed his backpack. He ran all the way to his bus stop. And then, because he was early, he ran down the block and back as many times as he could before the bus came.

When Max got to school, he told his best friend, Warren, about Mom's road-trip plans. "Cool!" said Warren. "But who is the Big Buckaroo?"

"That's my question too!" This was one reason Max and Warren were such good friends. They ate the same things and they liked to do the same things and most of the time they had the same questions about things too. "I think he is a movie-star guy," said Max.

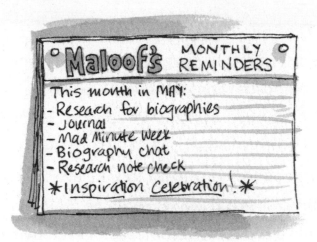

Maloof's MONTHLY REMINDERS

This month in MAY:
- Research for biographies
- Journal
- Mad Minute Week
- Biography chat
- Research note check
*Inspiration Celebration! *

"Maybe Mrs. Maloof has a biography about him," said Warren.

May was Biography Month in Mrs. Maloof's third grade, and the whole class had gone biography crazy. People were keeping lists of the books they had read and marking their favorites with smiley faces. In the beginning, every biography Max read had a smiley face beside it. Then he found *The Spine-Tingling Book of Awesome Explorers and Daring Discoveries* and erased all the other smileys.

The Spine-Tingling Book had seven biographies of seven awesome explorers. It had maps and charts and drawings and photos, plus long lists of Feats Accomplished and Discoveries Made. Max had read the whole book five times. Every time, he added another smiley face, and every time, his spine actually did tingle. When he thought about the Big Buckaroo, his spine didn't even twitch.

"Movie stars shouldn't get biographies," said Max. "Biographies are for people who do stuff. Movie stars just pretend to do stuff."

Max's classmate Glenn was standing nearby, eavesdropping like always. "Actors do stuff," said Glenn. "My mom's cousin was in a toothpaste commercial. She had to brush her teeth for six hours straight."

"Brushing your teeth for a commercial is different than brushing your teeth for real," said Max.

"It's still doing something," said Glenn.

Max wanted to say that it was not—not really—

but just then, Mrs. Maloof rang the Quiet Chime.

"Third-graders," said Mrs. Maloof, "I have an announcement."

Two announcements in one day? Max could hardly believe it.

Mrs. Maloof's announcements were more

unpredictable than Mom's. Sometimes they were about good things, like early-dismissal snow days, and sometimes they were about not-so-good things, like surprise geography quizzes or how Principal Adelle thought the noise level in the hallway was uncivilized. Max waited to see which kind of announcement this was before he got too excited.

"Biography Month has been a great success," began Mrs. Maloof. "I propose a celebration."

"Woo-hoo!" said Warren.

"Woo-hoo!" said Max. This *was* an exciting announcement. Celebrations in Mrs. Maloof's class meant watching movies and eating popcorn. Sometimes, there was extra recess.

"A *special* celebration," continued Mrs. Maloof. "An Inspiration Celebration."

"Will there be popcorn?" asked Max.

"I suppose we could have popcorn—but an Inspiration Celebration is different from the other celebrations we've had this year. Instead of our class watching a movie, we will be inviting guests to our classroom to watch all of *you*."

Max looked at Warren. Warren looked at Max. Maybe this wasn't such an exciting announcement after all.

"Each of you will give a speech about the most inspiring story you read during Biography Month."

Giving a speech about *The Spine-Tingling Book of Awesome Explorers and Daring Discoveries* was not quite as exciting as extra recess, but it was still pretty great. Max could tell about the maps and the photos. He could share about Feats Accomplished and Discoveries Made. He could mention all the ways that explorers were better than movie stars.

"Let's spend some time thinking about our speeches in our writer's notebooks," said Mrs. Maloof.

Max opened his notebook as fast as he could. At the top of the page, he wrote *THE SPINE-TINGLING BOOK OF AWESOME EXPLORERS AND DARING DISCOVERIES* in tall, blocky letters. His brain spun with spine-tingling thoughts. How was he going to get everything into one little speech?

While he thought, Max traced the letters on his notebook page. He liked how the *A* in *AWE-SOME* looked like a mountain peak. Max drew a patch of snow at the top and a tiny explorer

THE SPINE-TINGLING BOOK OF AWESOME EXPLORERS AND DARING DISCOVERIES

DRAWING BY: MAX LEROY!

climbing up the side. Then he made a scuba lady swim through one of the *O*'s in *BOOK*. A sailing ship threatened to crash into the *T* in *THE*. "Look out, Magellan!" Max shouted in his head. He imagined a miniature Ferdinand Magellan ordering his crew to let down the sails and steer away from the dangerous rocky title. "Follow us!" hollered Sacagawea. "We know a shortcut!"

Max was having so much fun drawing, he almost forgot he was still in Mrs. Maloof's classroom. His spine tingled. His toes tapped.

"Are you writing about a dancer?" said Glenn, looking at Max's tapping feet.

"I am writing about awesome explorers," said Max, even though it wasn't any of Glenn's business.

"Which one?" said Glenn.

"Not just one," said Max. "Seven."

"You can't do seven." Glenn pointed to the instructions Mrs. Maloof had written on the board.

"It says choose *a* biography. *A* means one."

Max's toes stopped tapping.

"*A*" did mean one.

Max looked at his drawings. He imagined all the tiny explorers looking back at him, hoping to be picked.

The tingling in Max's spine drained into his stomach and lumped there like cold oatmeal. How was he going to choose?

CHAPTER
THREE

Max thought about his explorers all afternoon. Even when he was supposed to be adding fractions. Even when he was supposed to be singing the Erie Canal song. Even during recess.

On the bus ride home, he opened *The Spine-Tingling Book* and looked at the pictures. Some of the explorers had photographs. Some of them lived in before-camera days, so there were only drawings. It didn't matter to Max. He loved looking at the pictures and imagining what the explorers were thinking. Usually, he imagined them saying something funny, like Fanny Workman saying, "You think climbing mountains is hard? Try doing it in a dress!" Or Sacagawea wish-

ing her husband wasn't such a showoff. Or Ernest Shackleton thinking, "Seal stew for lunch again?" But today, the explorers only seemed to say, "Pick me! Pick me!"

All of the Awesome Explorers were awesome. All of them deserved speeches.

How could he choose?

Max was still thinking about explorers when he got home from school, but when he walked into the kitchen, he stopped. Mom's always-tidy kitchen table was covered in papers and markers and craft supplies.

"Hooray! You're home!" said Mom. She looked almost as excited as she had when she told Max about her road-trip plans.

"Do you have another announcement?" asked Max.

"I have something fun for us to do. My cousin Merit is putting together a family album as a gift for Great-Great-Aunt Victory. He sent us each a scrapbook page to decorate. I thought we could have a crafting afternoon!"

Max and Mom used to have lots of crafting afternoons. They had made spiders out of egg  cartons and turtles out of walnut shells and once they even built a huge Bubble Wrap fort for Max's Stevicus action figure. When Mom started working at Shady Acres and taking nursing classes at the college, she had less time for crafting. The only thing he and Mom had made this year was  a clay porcupine for his Michigan Mammal project at school. A crafting afternoon did sound like fun.

Mom handed Max a scrapbook page. It was thick and square and very, very blank.

"Cousin Merit asked each of us to make a page about who we are and what we've done."

"Like Feats Accomplished and Discoveries Made," said Max.

"Cousin Merit suggested sharing hobbies and favorite snack foods, but feats and discoveries sound good too," said Mom.

Max sat down at the kitchen table. He grabbed a handful of markers. In his best printing, he wrote *MAX LeROY* on his scrapbook page.

When Max looked up, he saw that Mom had turned on her laptop and that his face was all over the screen. She had opened a file called MAX PIX, and in it were hundreds of photos. Max at his basketball games. Max in a Frankenstein costume. Max splashing at Stony Creek with Warren. There were pictures of holidays and birthdays and picnics and parades. There were even a few pictures of him and Dad in their sneaky spy disguises.

Mom showed Max how to print the pictures he wanted to add to his page. When they came out of the printer, he trimmed the edges and glued the backs and pressed them onto the thick white scrapbook paper.

Max imagined uncles and aunts and cousins gathering around to see his page. He wondered if they would look at the photos and know what he had been thinking. Just in case, he drew thought balloons coming out of each picture.

"Watch this layup!" said Basketball Max.

"Hope there aren't any sharks around," said At-the-Beach Max.

"Uhhhhhnnnnnnn . . ." moaned Frankenstein Max.

"Is being Frankenstein a feat or a discovery?" asked Mom.

"Both," said Max. "Because I discovered that it

is hard to walk in Frankenstein shoes—"

"But you did it anyway," said Mom.

"Yes," said Max. "With my feet. Get it? Feet? *Feat?*"

Mom laughed and shook her head, which made Max's spine tingle. He loved making Mom laugh.

"Is your page all finished?" asked Mom.

"Not yet." He had pasted a spy picture of himself with Dad in one corner of the page, but there was still something missing.

"I don't have any pictures of me and you," said Max.

"You don't?" Mom and Max scrolled through the MAX PIX file. There were plenty of pictures of Mom with Max when he was a baby, but the older Max got, the fewer pictures of Mom there were. And there were none from the past year. None at all.

"I guess *my* Discovery Made is that I'm always behind the camera these days instead of in front

of it." Mom shrugged in a way that was part *That's okay* and part not.

That gave Max an idea.

Max ran to his room and brought back the camera that he and Dad had used to take sneaky spy photos. He put his face next to Mom's and looked straight at the lens. *Snap!*

A picture of Max and Mom appeared on the screen. "Perfect," said Max.

"Oh, dear," said Mom. She smoothed her sproingy hair and ran her fingers through Max's curls. "Can we try one more?"

Max took another photo. *Snap!*

"Much better," said Mom. "Thanks, pal." Mom kissed Max on the cheek, and Max took another photo. *Snap!* This one made Mom laugh. *Snap! Snap! Snap!*

They took serious pictures and silly pictures and pictures with glitter glue on their fingers. They went outside and took a picture in front of the house and one by the apple tree they had

 planted in the backyard and one with their neighbor Mr. Yamamoto and his chameleon, Angus.

When they came back inside, Mom downloaded the photos into the computer and Max scrolled through them. All of the photos were great. But choosing the one he wanted for his scrapbook page was easy.

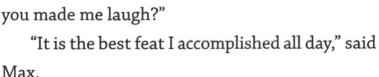

"Really?" said Mom. "You picked the one where you made me laugh?"

"It is the best feat I accomplished all day," said Max.

＊　＊　＊

Crafting afternoon had been so much fun that Max had forgotten all about his explorers. He did not think about them when he and Mom made room at the table so they could eat their lasagna, or when he helped Mom wash the dishes or when Mom scrolled through all the new photos in the MAX PIX file.

MAX PIX

"I like this one," said Mom. "You look so handsome—like a movie star."

A movie star? Max's stomach got the lumpy-oatmeal feeling again. He remembered the Big Buckaroo. And his conversation with Glenn. And how he was going to have to choose one explorer and leave out the rest. And he remembered a couple of other things too, even though he didn't want to.

"Is there something wrong?" asked Mom.

Max shook his head. Then he nodded. "How do you make a difficult decision?"

"That depends," said Mom. "What kind of difficult decision?"

Max told Mom about his explorers and how awesome they all were and how choosing one felt like saying the others weren't as good.

"Hmm," said Mom. Even though she and Dad did not live together anymore, they still did some stuff the same, like making a *hmm* sound when they were thinking hard about important things. "When I have that kind of difficult decision, I make a list."

Max was not surprised. Mom loved lists. The refrigerator always had two or three long yellow list papers stuck to it. Grocery Lists and Errand Lists and Don't Forget Lists.

Mom pulled her yellow list-making paper out from under a stack of scrapbooks. "I write down all the good and bad things about each of my options. For example, I've been trying to figure out where to stop for dinner on our way to Pennsylvania." She showed Max a page. There were restaurant names across the top. Under each name were notes about how far away it was and what kind of food it had and how much fun it would be to eat there.

"Which one did you choose?" asked Max.

"Well, each one had good points, but I wasn't sure what the deciding factor was . . . until just now." Mom circled the restaurant that had *FUN* written in big capital letters. "I had fun taking photos with you. I think for this trip, fun wins. What do you think?"

"I think I'd like to borrow some of that paper," said Max.

* * *

Max went to his bedroom. He turned to a fresh page in Mom's yellow list-making pad. At the top, he wrote all the explorers' names. Underneath, he listed their Feats Accomplished and Discoveries Made. He wrote down the cool things they did and the obstacles they overcame and how well they met their goals.

They were all pretty much the same. All of the explorers had cool facts and discoveries and feats. And all of them had reached their goals. Except Ernest Shackleton.

Shackleton's first big goal was to reach the South Pole before anyone else. But he didn't.

His second big goal was to walk across Antarctica, but he didn't do that, either. In fact, Shackleton's try at walking across Antarctica almost got him and his crew killed. Their ship got crushed by ice and they didn't have enough food or warm clothes and they almost froze.

Which was when Shackleton picked just a couple of guys and they got in a lifeboat and went looking for help. They paddled through ice storms and walked for days and climbed an ice mountain and had to slide down a huge snow cliff and could hardly take another step when they finally found a bunch of whaling guys. And then Shackleton went back with the whaling guys and rescued the rest of his crew. And nobody died. And nobody got left behind.

Max felt his spine tingle. He felt his toes tap.

He knew Ernest Shackleton was the right explorer for his Inspiration Celebration speech.

And he knew something else, too.

CHAPTER
FIVE

Max ran back into the kitchen. "I have an announcement," he said.

Mom set down her list-making pen. She gave Max her full attention. This made it a little harder for him to make his announcement, but he did it anyway.

"We can't leave Dad behind," said Max. "We have to bring him on our road trip."

Mom stayed quiet. Max stayed quiet too. Then Mom said, "Oh, kiddo. Have you been worrying about this all day?"

Max thought about it. He did not think he had been worrying about it, but maybe, some-place in his stomach, he had been.

"Sit." Mom pulled Max's chair up close to hers and patted it. Max sat. "You know Dad and I can't really go on vacation together anymore, right?"

Max didn't want to know, but he did. They had talked about this sort of thing when Dad had first moved out of the house and into a room at Grandma's. They had talked about it again when Dad had gotten his own apartment and when Max first went to spend the weekends there.

"It's one of those things that you guys aren't very good at anymore," said Max.

"That's true," said Mom. "But you know what is also true? We are both very, very good at loving you. We want you to do fun things, even when one of us can't be there to do them with you."

"Like how when I'm with Dad, you want me to

eat pizza and walk Ms. Tibbet's basset hounds?"

"I especially want you to walk basset hounds," said Mom.

"And Dad wants me and you to go see Great-Great-Aunt Victory and . . ."

"And Bronco Burt's Wild West arcade and the Big Buckaroo," said Mom. "Okay?"

"Okay," said Max. But he still did not feel all-the-way okay.

"Is there something else you want to talk about?" asked Mom.

Max nodded. There was something else . . . someone else. Someone handsome.

"What's so great about the Big Buckaroo?" said Max.

"The Big Buckaroo? What's *not* great?" Mom counted on her fingers. "Tall. Fast. Wild. Loopy."

Max understood why it might be good for a movie-star guy to be tall and fast and maybe even wild. But loopy?

"Wait. I have a picture." Mom sifted through the stacks of books and papers and craft supplies and pulled out a small red scrapbook. She put it in front of Max and opened it to the first page. There was a photograph of a girl with sproingy ponytails standing next to a painting of a cartoon horse. The horse had a sign on it that said HOLD IT, PARDNER! YOU MUST BE THIS TALL TO SADDLE UP!

"The Big Buckaroo is a horse?" said Max.

"Nope." Mom turned the page. There was a photo of the same girl sitting in a bright blue

seat with a bright blue bar across her lap. Next to the photo was a postcard of a tall, fast, wild, loopy roller coaster!

"The Big Buckaroo was the first roller coaster I ever went on," said Mom.

Big Buckaroo

Max looked at the picture of the girl. "That's you?" he said. Max knew that Mom used to be a kid, but most of the time he forgot. Most of the time, Mom seemed like she must always have been exactly the same as she was now.

"That's me," said Mom. "I was eight years old. And look—" She flipped back to the first photo. "I wasn't really tall enough to ride."

The girl in the photo was standing on her tiptoes, making her just tall enough to reach the measuring line on the sign. "You cheated!" said Max.

"I guess I did." Mom laughed.

"Do you think I'm as big as you were?" asked Max.

"In some ways, pal, you are a much bigger kid than I ever had to be." The way she said it made Max feel like he was a lot older than nine.

"Will you take a picture of me with the Big Buckaroo?" asked Max.

"Absolutely," said Mom. "Will you take one of me?"

Max nodded. He would take one of them together. "Can we send my picture to Dad?"

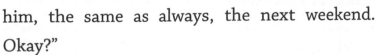

"Of course," said Mom. "And you'll see him, the same as always, the next weekend. Okay?"

Max thought about that. It was okay. Even Shackleton had to go away from his crew in order to come back and get them, right? That's what Max would do. He and Mom would go off and have their adventure and then Max would come home and tell Dad all about it.

That gave Max one more great idea.

He pulled out his scrapbook page. He found his black marker. Above the picture of himself and Mom, he drew one large thought bubble with two tiny bubble trails coming out of each of their heads. Inside the bubble he wrote, *Adventure, here we come!*

PART TWO

The Journey

CHAPTER
O N E

Max's spine tingled. His toes tapped. Only two more speakers, and then Mrs. Maloof would call him to the front of the room to read his speech.

Even though it was only the dress rehearsal for the Inspiration Celebration, Max was super excited. His Shackleton costume was perfect. His speech was perfect. Everything was perfect. The only thing that was not perfect was waiting his turn.

"Are you nervous?" asked Glenn. He was staring at Max's tapping toes.

"Explorers don't get nervous," said Max. He patted the name badge Mom had stitched onto his winter parka: MAXELTON, ANTARCTIC EXPLORER. He was wearing a pair of furry mittens he had found in the basement and some furry boots,

too. The boots were Mom's and kind of big and they made him walk funny, but Max did not mind. He figured that Antarctic explorers probably walked pretty funny themselves when they were trudging through the deep, deep snow.

Nope. Max was not nervous at all. But he was a little hot in his explorer gear. He unzipped his parka and put his mittens in his pocket with his speech. He waited. Only two more speakers.

At the front of the room, Zuri Gabriel was telling about Anna Pavlova, a ballerina from Russia who was such a good dancer that people named a dessert after her. Zuri did a tiptoe spin and held her speech paper high, so she had to tilt her head up to read it. "This summer I am going to have a ballet recital in my Uncle Teshome's garage."

That was the last line of her speech, Max knew. The line where she was supposed to say what sort of thing her biography person had inspired her to do. Mrs. Maloof called it the Declaration of Inspiration. Max's was *Someday, I am going to be a great explorer, just like Ernest Shackleton.*

Zuri spun again. The whole class applauded.

"Wow," said Warren.

"Wow," agreed Max.

"I'm going to moonwalk off stage," said Glenn, who was not applauding because he was holding his astronaut helmet with both hands. The helmet was part of an official astronaut suit that Glenn's mom had bought at an official gift shop from an official space museum. His name badge said GLENN because that was also the last name of the official astronaut Glenn's speech was about.

"Thank you, Zuri," said Mrs. Maloof. She said it in her best speaking voice because she was rehearsing too. In a dress rehearsal, everything was supposed to be exactly like it would be at the real performance. "Next, we will hear from Warren Sistrunk, who has selected Jacques Cousteau as his subject."

Max gave Warren a thumbs-up, because that was the kind of friends they were. He watched Warren walk to the front of the classroom. He was wearing a black turtleneck and a red knit cap and square swimming goggles. On his back he had a pretend oxygen tank that he and his dad had made out of a plastic soda bottle and some tubing.

Warren pretended to take a breath from his oxygen tank. "The most inspiring biography I read during Biography Month was called *Manfish*," he said. Warren sounded great. And his Declaration of Inspiration sounded even greater: "At camp this summer, I'm going to learn the backstroke." When his speech was over, Warren pretended to swim off stage.

"Wow," said Max. Now that Zuri had spun and Warren had swum, Max thought he should do something cool at the end of his speech too. Maybe he could pretend to walk through a blizzard? Or mush some invisible sled dogs?

"Thank you, Warren," said Mrs. Maloof. Her voice was sounding speechier with every introduction. "Next, Max LeRoy will tell us about the polar explorer Ernest Shackleton."

Finally! Max leaped from his seat. He zipped up his parka and put on his furry mittens and quick-walked to the front of the room as fast as his furry boots would let him. He knew his speech so well, he hardly had to look at his paper. "The best biography I read this month was about Ernest Shackleton," said Max. "He was an awesome explorer who tried to cross Artantica—" Wait. Did he just say . . .

"Art-ANTICA?" someone repeated. The class laughed.

Max's face turned red. His feet burned in his

furry boots. "I mean . . .
Art-*antica*." Argggh! He
said it again! The class
laughed even harder.

"That word is a tricky
one," said Mrs. Maloof.
She did not say it in her
dress-rehearsal voice. She
said it in her gentle voice,
which made everyone stop laughing. "Isn't it,
class?"

Probably Max's class was nodding, but Max
did not know that for sure. He was not looking at
the class. He was looking at his speech. The word
Antarctica stuck out, tall and mean and icy.

"Would you like to start over?" asked Mrs.
Maloof.

Max did not want to start over. He did not
want to risk saying *Art-antica* again.

He unzipped his parka.

He read the rest of his speech so fast, he forgot to say his Declaration of Inspiration.

When it was over, he walked back to his desk like a regular kid in too-big boots.

When Max got home from school, Mom was in the kitchen. The table was even messier than it had been during their crafting afternoon. But now, instead of scrapbook pages and glitter glue, the table was covered with maps and guidebooks and stacks of yellow list-making paper.

"Hey there, Max," said Mom. "How was school?"

Max shrugged.

Mom tapped a yellow list with her no-budge,

no-smudge ink pen. "I'm going to the market to-morrow after your Inspiration Celebration. Are there any last-minute things you need for our trip?"

Max shrugged again. There were a lot of minutes between now and after school tomorrow. How was he supposed to know if he needed any last-minute things when it wasn't the last minute yet?

"Okay," said Mom. She made another mark on her paper. "Let me know if that changes. By the time you get home from school, I want to be ready to hit the road. I'd like to do as much driving as I can before it gets dark."

Max knew Mom did not like driving in strange places in the super-dark night. And this gave him an idea. "We don't have to go to the Inspiration Celebration," he said. "We could skip school tomorrow and start our road trip in the morning."

"That's sweet of you, buddy. But I wouldn't

want to miss the Celebration. I've seen how excited you are about your speech."

Max did not feel sweet. And he did not feel excited. He felt like someone who would rather skip school than risk saying *Art-antica* again. He shrugged a third time, even though Mom hadn't  asked him any questions.

Mom looked at him the way he had seen her look at her having-a-hard-day patients. "You look like a kid who could use a snack." She lifted another yellow list. Underneath was a tin of homemade cookies. "I made them for the trip, but we should probably test them now. Chocolate chip," she said. "Cookie of champions."

"I'm not a champion," said Max.

"That's right," said Mom. "I forgot. You are an explorer. Well, I guess I'll just have to be the champion today." She took a cookie from the tin and bit into it. The chips looked melty and warm. "So," said Mom, "what do explorers have for a snack?"

The Spine-Tingling Book said Shackleton had packed lots of food for his journey, but when his ship sank and the food ran out, he and his crew had to eat whatever they could hunt. "Seal stew, mostly," said Max. "But I'm not an explorer, either."

"You're not?" Mom set down her cookie. "Did something happen at school today?"

Max did not want to say what happened, but he said it anyway. "I made a mistake during the dress rehearsal. I said *Art-antica.*"

"*Art-antica,* huh?" asked Mom. "Tricky word. Were you nervous?"

Max did not think he had been nervous before giving his speech. And he did not think he had been nervous when he'd said *Art-antica* the first time. But he was nervous now. The dress rehearsal was supposed to be exactly like the real speech. What if he said *Art-antica* during the real Inspiration Celebration? What if everyone laughed again?

"Do champions get nervous?" asked Max.

"Oh, sure," said Mom. "But we have a secret trick for dealing with it."

Max liked tricks. And he really liked secrets. "Is it super-secret?"

"Semi-super-secret," said Mom. "I'm pretty sure I could share it with you."

Max sat down beside Mom. He gave her his full attention.

"Okay," said Mom. "Step one: Take a deep breath."

Max inhaled deep.

"Step two: Let it out as slowly as you can."

Max let out his breath as slowly as he could— *Pfffuuuuuuuuh!*—while Mom counted. One. Two. Three. Four.

"Pretty good," said Mom, "for an explorer." She had a sparkly smile in her eyes, like she got when she challenged Max to a game of checkers. "Champions, of course, can hold their breath for a lot longer."

"Are you sure about that?" Max made sparkly challenge eyes too.

"Only one way to find out. Ready?" asked Mom.

"Ready!" said Max.

Max and Mom each took a deep breath.

Max let his breath out slow, slow, slowly. *Pff-fuuuuuuuh.*

Mom let her breath out slow, slow, slowly. *Pfffuuuuuuuh.*

They ran out of air at the exact same time.

"Rematch?" asked Mom.

"You're on," said Max.

Max and Mom took another deep breath.

Max let his breath out just a little. *Pffuh.*

Mom let her breath out just a little. *Pffuh.*

Then Max. *Pffuh.*

Then Mom. *Pffuh.*

Then Max. *Pffuh.*

Then Mom put her face very close to Max's and crossed her eyes. Max burst out laughing.

"I won!" said Mom.

"No fair!" said Max, but he kept laughing anyway.

"Feel better?" asked Mom.

Max thought about it. He did feel better. Mostly. "What do champions do if they get nervous in the middle of a speech? You can't breathe deep in the middle of a speech."

"Hmmmm," said Mom. "How about this? I'll sit in the front row. If you get nervous, you can give me a sign and I'll breathe deep for you."

"You think that will work?" asked Max.

"I think that you're going to do so well that you won't even need me. But if you do, I'll be there." She crossed her eyes again. "By the way, what was that word?"

"You mean *Antarctica*?" asked Max.

Mom leaned closer. "I'm sorry. I didn't hear that. What was the word?"

"*Antarctica*," said Max. "*Antarctica. Antarctica. Antarctica.*"

"Uh-huh." Mom took another bite of her cookie. "I'm sorry I don't have any seal stew for you."

Max pretended to be disappointed, but really he wasn't. He picked a cookie from the tin and took a big chocolatey bite.

"Not so bad being a champion, huh?" said Mom.

"Almost as good as being an explorer," said Max.

CHAPTER
THREE

When Max got to school the next morning, there was a banner hanging over his classroom door.

WELCOME TO OUR
INSPIRATION CELEBRATION!

"Third-graders," said Mrs. Maloof, "our special guests won't be here for another few hours. Until then, our day will be business as usual."

The business of the day did not feel very

usual. Everyone's spine seemed to be tingling. Everyone's toes seemed to be tapping. Zuri could not stop spinning. Glenn could not stop moonwalking. Even Warren did the backstroke from time to time. Whenever he could, Max practiced saying *Antarctica*. Whenever he needed to, he took deep breaths and let them out slow, slow, slowly.

At 11:45, Mrs. Maloof rang the Quiet Chime. "Time to get ready," she said.

The whole class sprang into action, rearranging desks and setting up rows of chairs for the special guests. Mrs. Maloof set juice boxes and bags of popcorn on the refreshment table.

Finally, it was time to put on their costumes.

Max zipped up his parka and slipped his feet into his too-big boots. He found his spot between Warren and Glenn just as the special guests began to arrive.

Usually, Mom was the first to arrive, but not today. Today, Zuri's Uncle Teshome was first. He sat in an aisle seat. "He has long legs," whispered Zuri. "He needs space."

Warren's parents arrived next. They sat at the back of the room with Warren's baby sister. "Uli sometimes fusses," explained Warren. "They might need to make a quick getaway."

Max watched the door as the seats filled. Finally, Mom appeared in the doorway, tucking a yellow paper into her purse and flattening her sproingy curls. She waved at Max and took a seat in the front row. Max did not tell Glenn and Warren why she sat in the front, but he knew.

Mrs. Maloof looked at the classroom clock just as Dad slipped in and stood behind Mr. Sistrunk. He saluted at Max. Max waved back.

"Special guests, it is a pleasure to welcome you to our Biography Month Inspiration Celebration," said Mrs. Maloof. Her voice was even speechier than yesterday.

Max took a deep breath. He let it out slow, slow, slowly as Mrs. Maloof introduced the first speaker.

He did it again when she introduced the second. And the third. And the fourth. Max studied his speech paper. *Antarctica,* he said in his head. *Antarctica. Antarctica. Antarctica.*

When it was Zuri's turn to speak, Max tried to listen, but mostly he could hear his own voice reminding him, *Antarctica. Antarctica.* He tried to breathe deep. He tried to let his breath out slow, slow, slowly.

"Are you okay?" asked Glenn.

"Pfffuuh," said Max.

Zuri spun and bowed. The special guests applauded.

Warren gave his speech and pretended to swim back to his spot next to Max. The special guests applauded again.

Then Mrs. Maloof stood. "Our next speaker is Max LeRoy, who will be sharing what he has learned about the polar explorer Ernest Shackleton," she said.

Max straightened his parka and put on his mittens. He shuffled his too-big boots to the front of the room. Warren gave him a thumbs-up. Dad saluted again. Mom took a deep breath.

Max held up his speech paper and began to read. "The best biography I read this month was about Ernest Shackleton. He was an awesome explorer who tried to cross"—he looked at Mom—"Ant-arc-ti-ca," said Max.

He had done it! Max could not help grinning. The audience grinned too, and some of them laughed, but not in a tricky-word way.

"I almost said *Art-antica*," Max explained. And then everyone laughed. Even Mom. Even Max.

The rest of his speech was perfect. Max told about all the ways Ernest

Shackleton was an awesome explorer. He told about Feats Accomplished. He told about Discoveries Made. He told about ice mountains and seal stew and the whole crew getting home safe. Then Max made his Declaration of Inspiration: "Someday I am going to be an awesome explorer, just like Ernest Shackleton."

The applause was so loud, Max did not worry about doing anything special at the end of his speech. The speech had been special enough. *Antarctica!*

* * *

When all the speeches were done, Max and his classmates joined their special guests for popcorn and juice.

"Great job," said Mom.

"Yeah, great job, champ," said Dad.

"Mom is the champ," said Max. "I am an explorer."

"Right," said Dad. "And I am a guy who has to

get back to work." He nodded to Mom. He hugged Max. "I'll see you next weekend," he said. "Have a great time on your trip. When you get back, I want to hear all about the grand expedition of Maxelton LeRoy."

The grand expedition of Maxelton LeRoy?

Max liked the way that sounded. He liked the way it made him feel. And most of all, he liked that it gave him a great idea. He did not have to wait until "someday" to be an awesome explorer like Ernest Shackleton. He could be an awesome explorer right now!

CHAPTER
FOUR

On the bus ride home, Max studied *The Spine-Tingling Book*. He had a lot of catching up to do if he was going to be an awesome explorer on this trip. After all, Mom had already declared their destination and charted their course and packed their provisions. When they got to Pennsylvania, Max could take over the discovering-things part, but he did not want to wait. There had to be some kind of awesome-explorer things he could do now.

Ernest Shackleton was a great leader, said the book. *He accomplished many feats and made many discoveries. He kept up his spirits and those of his crew, despite terrible hardships and deprivations.*

Even though Max had read *The Spine-Tingling Book* five times, he was still not sure what deprivations were, but he knew that hardships were like sleeping in a tent in the super-freezing cold and running out of food and walking a kabillion miles on the ice and not being able to feel your feet anymore.

It was only a block from Max's bus stop to his house, and the weather was warm and sunny, but Max put his shoes on the opposite feet for the walk home. It wasn't a super hardship, but it was a start.

* * *

When he got home, Max went straight to the kitchen. Mom was filling a cooler with snacks. "Which do you want for the trip?" She held up

 two yogurt cups. "Straw-
berry or blueberry?"

"Strawberry," answered
Max. He liked blueberry
best, which made straw-
berry more of a hardship.
It was too bad Mom didn't
have peach. He hated peach.

Mom put the strawberry yogurt in the cooler. She picked up a yellow list from the counter
and checked a box. "Done," said Mom. "Are you
all ready?"

Yesterday, she had given Max a yellow list
called MAX'S THINGS TO PACK. It had seemed like
a pretty good list when he was just a kid going
to his Great-Great-Aunt Victory's birthday party, but now that he was an awesome explorer, he
would need to make a few changes.

"Almost," said Max.

✳ ✳ ✳

Repacking his suitcase was not a hardship, but carrying it to the car was. Explorer gear was heavy! Max dragged his suitcase across the lawn. He heaved it into the trunk of the car. Now he was ready.

"All set, kiddo?" asked Mom.

"All set, *explorer*," corrected Max.

"Right. Explorer luggage in car—" Mom made a mark on her list. "Check. Explorer in car?"

Max leaped into the back seat and buckled his seat belt. "Check!" he said.

Mom slid into the front seat. "Porch light? Check. Door locked? Check. GPS set? Check."

Max's toes tapped. This must have been what Shackleton felt like when he was about to leave for Antarctica—except Max doubted that any of Shackleton's crew checked a box marked *Ask*

Shackleton if he needs to use the bathroom.

Finally, Mom set down her box-checking pen. "That's everything," she said. "Our first road trip together, just you and me." Mom looked at Max through the rearview mirror. "Are you ready, explorer?"

Max was more than ready. "Let's go, let's go!" he said.

*   *   *

Max watched the neighborhood pass by as Mom drove. He hoped the journey would be perilous. Lots of explorers had perilous journeys. And long ones too.

"What time is it?" asked Max.

"It's 4:30," said Mom.

"How long does it take to get to Pennsylvania?" asked Max.

"About six hours."

"Oh," said Max. Six hours was a lot shorter than the time it took Shackleton to sail from

England to Antarctica, but it was a lot longer than Max wanted to be in the car. He wished he had put some of his explorer things in the back seat instead of packing them all in his suitcase.

"Don't worry," said Mom. "It will go quick."

Max was not so sure. Mom always said that their grocery shopping would be quick, but it never was. Grocery shopping took forever.

"Here. This will help pass the time." Mom  handed Max a sheet of yellow list paper. At the top it said FUN THINGS TO DO ON THE ROAD. Underneath was a long list of games to play and songs to sing and things to think about.

"What is 'License Plate–Palooza'?" asked Max.

"You check the license plates of the cars that you pass and write down the states they are from and see if you can get all fifty."

Max looked out the window at the cars they passed.

Michigan.

Michigan.

Michigan.

Michigan.

All the license plates were from Michigan. Finally, Max saw a car from Ohio.

"Oooh!" said Mom. "Write it down!"

Max wrote it down. After a while, they saw a license plate from Indiana and wrote that down too. Mom's definition of *fun* was turning out to be a lot like her definition of *quick*.

Max looked at the list again. Maybe they should try a different game. "What is 'I'm an Animal'?"

"One person thinks of an animal, and the other person asks yes-or-no questions until he guesses what the animal is."

Max was good at I'm an Animal. It took him

only six questions to figure out that Mom was Mr. Yamamoto's pet chameleon, Angus. When Mom had to guess what Max was, it took her thirty-six questions. Then she gave up.

"I'm a blobfish," said Max.

"Excellent," said Mom. But she did not say it in a way that sounded like she thought it was excellent. She said it in a way that sounded like she was thinking of something else.

"Max," said Mom, "I'm going to turn on the radio for a minute, okay? I want to catch the weather report."

Max watched out the window while Mom listened to the weather report. He counted six Ohios and two more Michigans. Then Mom turned off the radio. "Hmmmm," she said.

That was her thinking-hard-about-something sound. "What?" asked Max.

"Nothing," said Mom. "There's a storm coming this way, that's all. Are you getting hungry?"

Max was getting hungry. He wished he had not said strawberry about the yogurt. "Yes. I guess."

"Good," said Mom. "Because we're almost there."

"Almost to Pennsylvania?" Maybe road trips were quicker than he thought.

Mom laughed. "No. We're almost to that restaurant I told you about. Remember? The fun one?"

Max did remember. Mom had circled it on her list. At the time, Max had been excited about going to a fun restaurant with Mom, but now that he had played License Plate–Palooza, he was not sure she could be trusted about what was fun and what wasn't.

* * *

Mom parked the car next to a building with big windows. Inside, Max could see people eating hot dogs. "Let's go, let's go!" said Mom.

"To the hot dog restaurant?" Max was surprised. Mom was not the kind of mom who took people to hot dog restaurants. Actually, Mom didn't go to restaurants much at all.

"Fun hot dogs," said Mom. "Famous hot dogs."

Max did not know how a hot dog could be famous. Then again, he did not know that a person could have a dessert named after them until yesterday.

Mom held open the door, and Max went

inside. At first it looked like a regular not-famous place. There were not-famous-looking people in booths and not-famous-looking waitresses and not-famous-looking photographs of chili dogs above the cash register. Then Max noticed the art on the walls.

"Are those hot dog buns?" asked Max.

Mom grinned. "Famous hot dog buns. Signed by famous people."

Max looked at the hot dog buns. There were hundreds of them, mounted on wood and covered with plastic. Each bun had a fat black signature on it and a tiny gold plaque underneath that told who the signer was.

Max read the names aloud. Margaret Thatcher. Alan Alda. Danny Glover. Who were these people? "Art Garfunkel?" said Max. Was that a real name? It sounded as mixed up as saying *Art-antica*.

Finally, he found a name he recognized. "John Glenn," said Max. "If Glenn were here, he would be excited."

"Are you excited?" asked Mom.

"I'm hungry," said Max.

"Me too," said Mom.

"Dining in or taking out?" asked a lady in an apron. Her name tag said MILLIE.

Mom turned to Max. "I had planned for us to eat here, but with the storm coming, I think we should take out and get back on the road, okay?"

Max nodded. "Okay."

"Well, now that that's decided, what'll you have?" asked Millie.

"What did Art Garfunkel have?" asked Max. He didn't really care about the answer. He just wanted to say Art Garfunkel again.

"Wouldn't know," said Millie. "That was before my time here. I did meet a gymnastics girl. And a golfer, and a couple of those TV-talent-show kids."

Mom ordered some hot dogs and some

lemonade and sides of pickles and fries.

"Did you ever meet an explorer?" Max asked Millie while they waited for their order.

"Don't think so," said Millie.

"I'm an explorer," said Max.

"That so?"

"I'll sign a bun if you want."

"I wouldn't mind, but the owners are really looking for famous people. Are you famous?"

"Not yet," admitted Max.

"Well, come back when you are," said Millie. She reached into her apron pocket and pulled out a coupon. "Bring this and you'll get a free dessert, too."

Max took the coupon. Free dessert sounded almost as good as signing a hot dog bun. Maybe, if he got really famous, they would even name the dessert after him.

When their order came up, Millie handed the drinks to Mom and the bags of hot dogs and pickles and fries to Max. "You drive safe," she said. "And be sure to check out Barack Obama and Joe Biden's buns on your way out."

Max knew what Millie meant, but it still sounded funny to be told to check out a president's buns.

Max tried not to laugh. He looked at Mom. She did not look like she was trying not to laugh. She looked like she was trying to get to the car as quickly as she could.

CHAPTER FIVE

As soon as they got in the car, Max took a hot dog out of the bag. He held it out to Mom.

"You eat," said Mom. "I'm not hungry right now."

Max saw Mom look out at the sky. It was getting dark. Was it late already?

"What time is it?" asked Max.

"What?" asked Mom. "Oh, 6:20."

Mom pulled out of the parking lot and into traffic. All around, the sky grew darker, but not in a soft, slow, night-is-coming way. In a gray-green-crackly sort of way.

Raindrops plinked on the windshield. Then they plunked. The air in the car felt spiky and sharp.

"The weather report said there was only a chance of showers," said Mom. "Guess we're getting the chance." Her voice was spiky and a little sharp too. Max looked out the window. Trucks whizzed by. "Oklahoma!" said Max. "I saw an Oklahoma license plate."

"Max, I need to concentrate on the road." Max saw Mom tighten her grip on the steering wheel.

The rain came harder. The sky grew darker and greener and the air felt even more crackly. It was too dark to read the list of FUN THINGS TO DO ON THE ROAD and too crackly to do any of them anyway.

The rain slapped. Sometimes there was lightning. Thunder rattled the cups in the cup holders.

Mom drove and drove and drove.

After a very long time, the slapping slowed. The sky wasn't quite so green and so dark. Off in the distance, Max saw a streak of blue.

But Mom's hands were tight on the steering wheel. The air was still crackling around her. In the rearview mirror, Max could see her eyes. They looked a little like she had just said *Art-antica* in front of her whole class.

Max took a deep breath. He let it out slow, slow, slowly. *Pffffffffuh.*

Mom's eyes met his in the mirror. He took another deep breath. Mom did too. *Pfffuuuuuuuuh.*

"Thanks, pal," said Mom. Her eyes did not look Art-antic-y any longer, but she still sounded sharp. "I hate driving in weather like this."

"It is a hardship," agreed Max.

The Spine-Tingling Book said that during some hardships, Shackleton kept spirits up by getting his men to put on plays and sing songs. He even had a guy in the crew who could play the banjo. Max did not have a banjo. He did have a harmonica, but it was packed in his suitcase with the rest of his explorer gear. He did not think he could put on a play right now, either. How could Mom watch when her eyes were on the road?

Then Max got an idea.

"Hey, Mom, can I ask a question?"

"It is seven o'clock," said Mom.

"Okay," said Max. "But that wasn't my question."

"Oh," said Mom. "I'm sorry. What's your question?"

"Why didn't the skeleton ride the roller coaster?"

Max thought he saw the corners of Mom's mouth twitch. "I don't know, Max. Why didn't the skeleton ride the roller coaster?"

"Because he didn't have the guts."

Mom smiled. "Good one." Her voice was a little less sharp than before.

"Hey, Mom?"

"Yes, Max?"

"Why didn't the rooster go on the roller coaster?"

"Tell me."

"Because he was a chicken."

Mom smiled wider.

"Hey, Mom?"

"Yes, Max?"

"Why didn't the magician take his hat off on the roller coaster?"

"Why?"

"Because he didn't want to get his hare messed up. Get it? Hair? *Hare?* Like a rabbit."

This time Mom laughed. "I get it," she said.

The car was completely crackle-free, but Max had a few more jokes to tell.

"Why didn't the octopus go on the roller coaster? Because he was spineless! Why didn't the clock go on the roller coaster?"

"Let me guess . . ." said Mom. "Because he was out of time?"

"Because he was alarmed!" said Max. Then he thought of another one. "Hey, Mom? Why didn't the polar explorer go on the roller coaster? Because he got cold feet!"

Mom turned off the windshield wipers. The sky was nearly blue. "Hey, Max?"

"Yeah, Mom?"

"How did the kid in the back seat get to be so good at road trips?"

"I don't know," said Max.

"I don't know either, but I'm glad he did." Mom reached over the back of the seat and put out her hand. Max held it. "You are a sweet kid." Mom squeezed his hand. "But right now, I'm looking for a hot dog." Max gave Mom a hot dog.

"Thanks, champ—no, wait. I know. You're not a champ; you're an explorer. An awesome explorer."

"And you are an awesome champion," said Max.

"Thanks," said Mom.

Mom kept driving. They played games and sang songs and thought thoughts. Slowly, the sky slipped from light blue to medium blue to soft almost-dark.

PART THREE

Feats Accomplished and Discoveries Made

CHAPTER
ONE

"Max?" said Mom. "Where are all your clothes?"

Max opened one eye. It was morning. He was in a motel room in a cushy bed with cozy blankets. Rats! He had planned to spend the night on the floor for more hardship.

"Did I fall asleep in the car?" asked Max.

"You were so sleepy, you crawled into bed without changing into pajamas. Did you know your shoes were on the wrong feet?"

"Explorers have hardships and deprivations," said Max.

"Too bad they don't have clean shirts," said Mom. Max's suitcase was open on Mom's bed, and his explorer gear was spread out around it. "What happened to all the clothes on the list I gave you?"

"Explorers make sacrifices," said Max.

"I see," said Mom. "I'm not sure I'd have sacrificed clean socks to make space for a collapsible fishing pole."

"That's the difference between explorers and moms," said Max.

"That, and moms have something to wear today," said Mom. That was when Max noticed.

Mom was not wearing the jeans and sneakers she wore at home. She was not wearing the nurse clothes and soft white shoes she wore to work at Shady Acres, either.

What Mom was wearing was a pink skirt Max had never seen before and shoes that showed her toes. Her toes had pink polish on them. *Did they always have pink polish on them?* Max wondered. The biggest wonder of all was what had happened to her hair. Mom's sproingy curls were gone! Her

hair was smooth and swoopy and the ends seemed sharp.

"How do I look?" asked Mom.

"You look pink," said Max, which was not exactly what he was thinking. What he was exactly thinking was that Mom did not look like Mom at all.

But she still sounded like Mom. "And you look like a boy who slept in his clothes."

Max had not slept in all of his clothes. On Mom's bed was his jacket with all the pockets. Max filled the pockets with all the explorer things that would fit and zipped them shut.

"An explorer is always prepared," said Max.

* * *

While Mom drove to Bronco Burt's, Max flipped through the pages of *The Spine-Tingling Book* until he reached his favorite photo. In it, Ernest Shackleton stood in the polar snow, his foot up on an ice chunk. He looked tall and brave and awesome. Under the picture was the Shackleton family motto: *By Endurance We Conquer*.

There was another guy in the photo too, hunching in the whippy white snow. He did not look tall or brave or awesome. He looked like a guy whose family motto might be *Let's Go Home and Eat Soup*.

"Hey, Mom?" said Max. "Do we have a family motto?"

"How about *If There Is Bad Traffic Around, We Will Find It*."

Max knew this was supposed to be a joke. He laughed a little so Mom would not feel bad. "But really, do we have a family motto?" he asked again.

"I don't know," said Mom. "But a family reunion is a great place to find out."

Max had almost forgotten they were headed to a family reunion, mostly because he had been thinking about being an explorer and second mostly because he had been thinking about riding rides and playing games and snacking on snacks. Besides, Grandma was the only Pennsylvania family he really knew, and she was staying in Florida until the summer. How could he *re*union with the people in his family if he didn't even remember *union*ing in the first place?

"Are you sure I've met Great-Great-Aunt Victory before?" asked Max.

"I showed you the picture, remember? The one that made my uncles call you Spooner?" Max did remember seeing the picture. He just didn't remember the uncles.

"Don't worry. Our Pennsylvania family is very nice, and they will be very happy to see you again."

Max watched as Mom smoothed her hair. She smoothed it again when they parked in the Bronco Burt's lot. She put on pink lipstick, too. When she saw Max watching, she said, "Explorers aren't the only ones who get prepared."

Max guessed not. But he was glad explorer preparing did not include putting on lipstick.

CHAPTER
TWO

Bronco Burt's Wild Ride Amusement Park was amazing! As soon as they walked through the gate, Max saw spinny rides and bumpy rides and rides that rattled and rolled. He smelled sweet things and salty things and things that he knew had been fried and rolled in cinnamon. Everywhere he looked, there was something new to explore.

"Look!" Mom pointed high above a line of trees. "The Big Buckaroo!" Blue steel tracks rose like a mountain and then fell into a double loop-de-loop. Max watched as a coaster car climbed the highest peak, paused, then dove and looped, dove and looped. The people on the car screamed wild, happy screams.

"Let's go, let's go!" Max started to run, but Mom did not. She pulled a piece of paper from her skirt pocket.

"Cousin Merit sent instructions. We're supposed to head straight to the Okey Doke Corral for the Family Meet-and-Greet."

"Then we'll go on the Big Buckaroo?" asked Max.

Mom checked the paper. "Then we'll get a schedule of reunion events," she said. "But don't worry, pal. You'll ride that coaster, one way or the other."

* * *

Max did not think the Okey Doke Corral looked much like a corral. There weren't any horses or

guys having Wild West shootouts. Mostly, there was grass and picnic tables and a tall white tent with a banner that said HAPPY 100TH, VICTORY! Some of the picnic tables had banners too. They said things like SCRAPBOOK STATION and HATCHECK and FAMILY TREE. Everywhere Max looked, there were people in cowboy hats.

Mom looked at her instructions again. "I'm supposed to sign in at the hatcheck table, but you can explore a little if you want. Just don't go too far."

Exploring sounded good. Max unzipped one of his pockets and took out his magnifying glass. He didn't really need it in order to see the tall, tall mountain of the Big Buckaroo, but it was fun to look through.

Another coaster car had climbed to the peak. Max could almost make out the people on the ride. He wondered if any of them were looking back at him.

"Excuse me." Max felt a tap on his shoulder. He turned around. Through his magnifying glass, he saw a girl who looked like she had an enormous chin, but when he put the glass down, her chin turned out to be regular-size after all. She was wearing a cowboy hat and a T-shirt that said PICKLER'S AUTO PARTS. "Excuse me," she said again. "I'm looking for all the Picklers. Are you a Pickler?"

"No," said Max. "I'm an explorer."

"Weird," said the girl. "Hey, Dad!" she shouted to a man standing behind the Family Tree table. He had on the same T-shirt as the girl, but in a bigger size. "This kid says he's an Explorer!"

"Weird," said the man. He waved Max over. "Your name is Explorer?"

Max shook his head. "My name is Max. I *am* an explorer. It's, like, my job."

"Wow," said the girl.

"Nice to meet you, Max," said the man. "What's your last name?"

"LeRoy," said Max.

"LeRoy . . . LeRoy . . . I saw a LeRoy . . ." The man ran his hand across a long white paper that covered the entire picnic table. On it were dozens of tiny names with thin black lines connecting one to another. "Le . . . Roy . . ."

"I'm a Pickler," said the girl. She pointed to a name on the paper. Max used his magnifying glass to read it: *Constance Pickler*. "You can call me Connie." Connie pointed to two other names. "That's my older brother Royal Pickler and my *older* older brother, Frank Pickler Jr. And these"—she traced a thin black line to two other names—"are my parents, Miranda Pickler and Frank Pickler Sr."

"LeRoy!" said Frank Sr. "There! Max LeRoy. Is that you?"

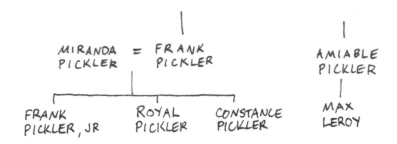

MIRANDA PICKLER = FRANK PICKLER

AMIABLE PICKLER

FRANK PICKLER, JR   ROYAL PICKLER   CONSTANCE PICKLER

MAX LEROY

Max looked at the place where Frank Sr. was pointing. There was his name: *Max LeRoy.*

A thin black line connected his name to one Max had never seen before: *Amiable Pickler.*

"Is that your mom or your dad?" asked Connie.

Max looked at the name again. It did not belong to his mom or his dad. Could there be two Max LeRoys on this family tree?

"There you are, Max." Max turned around. Mom had two cowboy hats. She set one on Max's head, then smoothed her hair and put on the other. "Reunion rule: Everyone must wear hats. That way we know who is family and who is not."

"Are you Amiable?" Connie asked Mom.

"Only after I've had my coffee."

Max could tell Mom was joking, but even if he had understood the joke, he would not have laughed. He was too busy being surprised. As long as Max had known Mom, she had been Amy LeRoy. That was how she signed permission slips. That was how she had introduced herself to Mrs. Maloof on the first day of school. Max had never heard Mom call herself Amiable. And he had never not heard her call herself a LeRoy. Max was a LeRoy. Dad was a LeRoy. LeRoy was how people knew who Max's family was, even if they weren't all wearing the same hat.

"Amy? Is that you?" Another man rushed up to the table.

"Cousin Merit!" Suddenly, Mom was surrounded by cowboy-hatted people.

"And this must be Spooner!" said Cousin Merit.

Max wanted to say it must *not* be, but he didn't. "I'm Max," he said.

"He's an explorer," explained Connie.

Cowboy-hatted people surrounded Max, too. There was a lot of hugging and shaking hands and cheek-kissing.

"Ugh," said Max.

"Double ugh," said Connie. "Let's get out of here. My dad said my brothers and I could go on the rides for a while. You guys want to come?"

Max escaped another cheek kiss and nodded. He tugged on Mom's arm. "Let's go," he said.

Mom's face looked like it sometimes did when

Dad came to pick Max up for the weekend. Sort of sad, but sort of business-y. "I asked at the hat-check if we had a family motto. The woman there said it was probably *If It Isn't on the Schedule, It Doesn't Exist.*"

Mom showed Max a piece of paper with the words REUNION SCHEDULE at the top. The whole day was planned out to the minute. There were times for family stories and times for taking photos and times for doing crafts and times for singing songs. Max did not see any times written down for riding rides or going to the arcade or looping the loop of the Big Buckaroo.

"Sorry, pal," Mom said. "I'm stuck."

"Max could come with us," said Connie. "He can be an honorary Pickler."

"What do you think?" asked Mom.

What Max thought was that he did not want to be a Pickler, even if it was honorary. But he did want to go on the rides. He wished Mom could go too. "Don't you want to ride the Big Buckaroo?" asked Max.

"Explorers aren't the only ones who have to make sacrifices," said Mom. "You go and have fun. Be back by noon, okay?" She showed Max and Connie the NOON line on the Reunion Schedule. Next to it, it said BIRTHDAY CAKE.

"Double okay!" said Connie. She grabbed Max's arm, and they were off and running before Max could even say goodbye.

CHAPTER THREE

"This is our cousin Max," Connie told her brothers. They were wearing cowboy hats too, and the same auto parts T-shirt as Connie and her dad. "Max is an explorer. It's his job."

"I wish I had a job," said Royal. "Frank Jr. is a paperboy, but Connie and I are nothing."

Max thought about that. Shackleton explored with a whole crew. If Max was going to explore Bronco Burt's with his cousins, they should have jobs too.

Max handed Royal a map that he and Mom had picked up at the park entrance. "You can be the navigator. When I name a destination, you will tell us how to get there."

"Cool," said Royal. "I'm good at telling people where to go."

Max unzipped another pocket, pulled out his explorer camera, and gave it to Frank Jr. "And you can be our photographer. You can document our expedition."

"Double cool," said Frank Jr. "I'm good at documenting."

"What can I be?" asked Connie.

"You can be the first mate," said Max. "That's the next-to-the-top guy. If ever I can't lead, you have to take over."

"I'm good at taking over," said Connie.

"Triple cool," said Max, because it was triple cool. Not only was Max an explorer; now he had a crew!

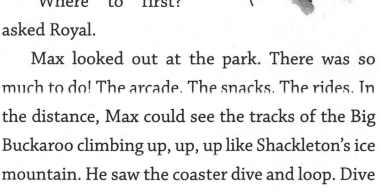

"Where to first?" asked Royal.

Max looked out at the park. There was so much to do! The arcade. The snacks. The rides. In the distance, Max could see the tracks of the Big Buckaroo climbing up, up, up like Shackleton's ice mountain. He saw the coaster dive and loop. Dive and loop. He heard the wild, happy screams.

Max's spine tingled. He stood tall and brave and awesome. If there had been an ice chunk around, he would have put his foot up on it. "Our final destination will be the summit." He pointed at the Big Buckaroo. "But first, we will accomplish many feats and make many daring discoveries. There will probably be hardships and deprivations, too. Are you prepared?"

"We are prepared," said the cousins in very crew-like voices.

"First stop, the Twister." Max had noticed the Twister when he and Mom entered Bronco Burt's. It had up-and-down arms and round-and-round cars and a floor that tilted like a spinny top. Max had never been on a ride like it. Maybe it could count as a daring discovery?

Royal studied the map. "The Twister. Two lefts, then a right at High Noon Hot Dogs," he said.

Max and his crew quick-walked to the Twister. "Excellent navigating," said Max.

"Thank you," said Royal.

Frank Jr. snapped a photo.

"Excellent documenting," said Max.

"Thank you," said Frank Jr.

The Twister operator opened the gate to the ride.

"Follow me," said Max. He led them to the car that looked the spinniest, and they all piled inside.

"I did excellent following," said Connie.

"Yes, you did," said Max.

"Thank you," said Connie.

The Twister took off. Max was right. Their car was the spinniest. And the fastest. And the most awesome.

"That was great!" said Connie. "What's next, Fearless Leader?"

Fearless Leader? *The Spine-Tingling Book* did not say that Shackleton got called Fearless Leader, but Max liked it anyway. It made him feel tall. "The Dizzy Dust Bowl," said Max.

"This way," said Royal.

* * *

All morning long, Max led fearlessly. He and his crew rode spinny rides and bumpy rides and rides that rocked and rolled. They played games at the arcade and ate snacks at the snack bars. Royal navigated. Frank Jr. documented. Connie did her best not to take over, but Max could tell it was not easy.

"What time is it?" asked Connie.

Max looked up. The sun was almost directly overhead. "My explorer skills tell me it is almost noon," said Max.

"So does my watch," said Royal.

"Next stop, the Big Buckaroo!" said Connie.

"I think the Fearless Leader is supposed to say that," said Frank Jr.

"I know," said Connie. "But I'm right, right?"

"Right," said Max. "To the Big Buckaroo!"

Royal navigated. Frank Jr. snapped. Connie followed.

Max led, keeping his eye on the Big Buckaroo. With every step, the coaster grew taller. And faster. And loopier. The screams of the riders sounded less and less like wild, happy screams and more like plain old screams.

By the time they reached the HOLD IT, PARD-NER! sign, Max did not feel fearless at all. An oat-mealy lump had formed in his throat.

"Time to measure up," said the roller coaster man. Frank Jr. stood in front of the painted horse, just like Mom had in her scrapbook photo. He was plenty tall. Royal was plenty tall too. Connie stood on her tiptoes, but the roller coaster man didn't notice.

"Next!" he called.

Max stepped in front of the painted horse. He took off his cowboy hat. He flattened his hair. He did not stand tall and brave and awesome. He stood sort of hunched, like a guy who wanted to go home and eat soup.

"Want me to take a picture?" asked Frank Jr.

"No, thank you," said Max.

"You're in, pardner," said the roller coaster man.

Slowly, Max climbed the steps to the platform where the Big Buckaroo cars were and joined his cousins in line. His spine was not tingling. His toes were not tapping. The lump in his throat had slid down into his stomach and was getting bigger every minute.

"Next!" cried the roller coaster man. Max watched as the people in front of them filled a coaster car. "Seat belts on! Safety bar in place!" the coaster man told them. He pushed a button, and Max saw the cold blue car jolt forward. "Hold on to your hats!" yelled the man.

"I'm not holding my hat when we ride," said Connie. "I'm holding on to the safety bar."

"You have to hold your hat," said Frank Jr. "Otherwise it will fly off during the ride and you'll never get it back."

This gave Max an idea. A very good idea. He made his voice sound fearless, even if he wasn't. "Crew," he said, "you must go to the summit alone. I will stay behind and hold on to our hats."

"Are you sure?" asked Royal.

"Explorers make sacrifices," said Max.

"Wow," said Frank Jr.

"Double wow," said Royal.

"I'm in charge!" said Connie.

Connie collected the hats and handed them to Max. She ordered her brothers into their coaster car. She sat down behind them and pulled the safety bar down tight. "Ready!" she called to the roller coaster man.

Max watched their car rickety-click up the tall

and terrible summit. He tried to stand tall and brave and awesome, just in case any of the cousins looked back, but they did not. His oatmealy feeling grew bigger and bigger, even as he heard his cousins' wild, happy screams.

CHAPTER
FOUR

Max let Connie lead them back to the Okey Doke
Corral and into the big white tent. There, he
found a small stage and many rows of chairs filled
with cowboy-hatted people. But he could not find
Mom.

"Want to sit with us, Fearless Leader?" asked
Connie.

Max shook his head. He did not feel like a
fearless leader. And he did not feel like an explorer with a crew. He felt like a kid who wished his

mom would take off her cowboy hat so he could find her.

"Max! Max!" Max heard Mom's voice. There she was! Standing in the front row. Max should have known.

"You're just in time!" Mom patted the seat beside her, and Max sat in it. "That is your Great-Great-Aunt Victory."

Up on the stage was a big red chair like a queen would sit in, but instead of a queen, there sat an old, old woman in an old, old cowboy hat. Her face was even more wrinkly than Dad's neighbor Ms. Tibbet's, and she sat up very tall and straight— almost as tall and straight as Shackleton.

On either side of her stood a cowboy-hatted man. One had a microphone. The other pushed a wheely cart with an enormous birthday cake on it. Max could not tell if there were one hundred candles on it, but it looked like it. He could feel the heat of them from the front row.

"Victory would like to invite all the children to help her blow out her candles," said the microphone man.

Max did not want to go on stage. He wanted to stay with Mom. But when Connie ran by, she tugged his arm.

"Go ahead," said Mom.

Max went on stage and stood beside the cake.

"One . . . two . . . three . . . blow!"

Great-Great-Aunt Victory blew. The children blew. Every flame went out.

Max took a step back toward Mom, but the microphone man stopped him. "While the cake is being cut, do any of the children have a question for Victory?"

Connie raised her hand. "What did you wish for?" she asked.

"I wished for cake," said Great-Great-Aunt Victory.

Other kids asked questions too, about how it felt to be so old and what she remembered about being a kid and whether she liked her cake plain or with ice cream. Then the microphone man turned to Max.

"And what about you, young sir? Is there

something you'd like to know?"

There was something Max wanted to know. "Do we have a family motto?" he asked.

"A family motto?" said the man.

"Like Ernest Shackleton's family motto was *By Endurance We Conquer*. And a hat lady said our family motto was probably *If It Isn't on the Schedule, It Doesn't Exist*." The audience chuckled, but Great-Great-Aunt Victory did not laugh. She sat even straighter in her chair.

"I don't know about family mottoes," said Great-Great-Aunt Victory. "But I do have my own."

"You do?" said Max. "What is it?"

"*Ignore All Mottoes*," said Great-Great-Aunt Victory.

* * *

When Max went back to sit with Mom, Connie followed. "We forgot to give you back your explorer stuff." She handed Max his map and his camera.

"Did you kids have a good time?" asked Mom.

Connie took back the camera and turned it so Mom could see the pictures Frank Jr. had taken. "That's us by the Twister and that's us eating hot dogs and that's us at the ring toss and that's just the ground, but that's me and Royal on the Big Buckaroo. And that's Max looking up at us."

Mom looked at the picture. Then she looked at Max. "You didn't go on the Big Buckaroo?"

"I led that expedition," said Connie. "Max stayed behind and held on to our hats."

"Explorers make sacrifices," said Max. He wished his voice sounded a little more fearless.

"Maybe that could be your family motto!" said Connie. Then she headed off for cake.

"I like Great-Great-Aunt Victory's motto better," said Mom.

"Do you like it more than the one about schedules?"

"Especially more than the one about schedules." Mom took off her cowboy hat. Her hair had gotten a little sproingy. Max took off his hat too. "The schedule says I'm supposed to join the family sing-along next, but . . ." Mom slid the Reunion Schedule under her seat and she slid both their hats under their seats too. "Let's go, let's go," she whispered.

* * *

All afternoon, Max and Mom rode rides and played games and snacked on snacks. Max showed Mom the spinniest car on the Twister and the dustiest spot in the Dizzy Dust Bowl and how to hit the trickiest targets at Annie O's Shoot-'Em-Up Gallery. They explored the park from one end to the other. Finally, Mom said, "Max, I don't know how much more walking I can do in these silly shoes."

Max understood. His feet still felt a little weird from wearing his shoes on the wrong feet yesterday.

"I think I can manage one more ride. What'll it be, explorer?"

Max looked at Mom. Then he looked up, up over her head to the tall, tall tracks of the Big Buckaroo. Max swallowed hard, but he did not notice any oatmeal lumps in his throat. There weren't any in his stomach, either. In fact, his spine was tingling.

"How about the Big Buckaroo?" said Max.

"I thought you'd never ask," said Mom.

Max and Mom walked as fast as her toe-

showing shoes could go. When they reached the HOLD IT, PARDNER! sign, Mom borrowed Max's explorer camera. "Ready for your close-up?"

Max fluffed up his hair. He stood tall and brave.

"Awesome," said Mom. "We'll send this one to your dad."

"Would you like one of the two of you together?" asked the roller coaster man.

Max and Mom posed in front of the painted sign. Max stood on his tiptoes, even though he didn't need to. The roller coaster man snapped the photo and handed the camera back to Max. "Ready to ride?" he asked.

Max and Mom ran up the steps to the platform. Max hopped up and down as he waited. Mom bounced a little too.

The next coaster car rolled in. Max and Mom sat right in the front. They buckled their seat belts. They pulled the safety bar down tight.

"Hold on to your hats!" the roller coaster man announced, but since Max and Mom weren't wearing any hats, they didn't have to worry about that.

The car lurched forward. *Rickety-clickety, rickety-clickety.* Up, up, up they went, up the tall, tall tracks of the Big Buckaroo.

"I remember the first time I rode this coaster. I was so scared, I didn't let go of the safety bar for one second," said Mom.

"Are you scared now?" asked Max.

"Maybe a little. It has been a very long time," said Mom.

Max did not hold on to the safety bar, but he did hold on to Mom's hand. "So you aren't scared," he explained.

Rickety-click, rickety-click . . . Up, up, up they went. When they reached the summit, Max looked around. He could see the whole park. The Twister. The arcade. Far in the distance, he could even see the Okey Doke Corral, though the people looked so small, he could not tell which ones were wearing hats and which ones weren't.

He started to wonder what Shackleton had seen from the top of his ice mountain when—*whoosh!* The Big Buckaroo dove and looped, dove and looped! Max could see that Mom was laughing a wild, happy scream, but he could not hear her because he was happy-screaming too.

CHAPTER
FIVE

Max and Mom rode the Big Buckaroo five more times before it really was time to go back to the Okey Doke Corral. Mom walked as fast as she could in her toe-showing shoes, but that was not very fast. This gave Max time to think. He had had a great day. He had explored a lot. But he hadn't really discovered anything except for Mom's name, which didn't seem like a daring discovery. But it did seem daring to ask her about it.

"How come you say your name is Amy when it

isn't?" asked Max.

"Do you know what Amiable means?" asked Mom. "It means 'likable.'"

"You are likable," said Max.

"Thank you," said Mom. "You are likable too. But I don't want you to *have* to be likable. When your name is Amiable, everyone expects you to be pleasant. All the time. Even when you might be angry or scared or bored—"

"Or making sacrifices," said Max.

"Exactly. It is impossible to live up to. So I shortened Amiable to Amy."

Max understood. Principal Adelle expected them to be quiet and civilized, even in the gym, even on the playground. Max could only imagine how much worse it would be if his name were Quiet LeRoy or Civilized LeRoy.

"Does LeRoy mean anything?" asked Max.

"I think it means 'the king,'" said Mom.

"Is being the king impossible to live up to

too?" asked Max. "Is that why the Family Tree said Amiable Pickler?"

"It said Pickler?" asked Mom.

"Yes," said Max.

"Wow," said Mom. "It must have felt weird to see that."

Max did not think it had felt weird, but he did not think he knew the word for what it did feel like either, so he just said yes.

"Max, Frank Sr. filled out the family tree information, not me. Pickler was my last name before I married your dad and became a LeRoy. I guess because your dad and I aren't together anymore, Frank wrote Pickler instead."

"So you're still a LeRoy. Like me. And like Dad. Like our whole family."

Mom stopped walking. Max thought it was because her feet were hurting, but then she squatted down and looked Max straight in the eye. She might have had strange swoopy hair and

new shoes and a new skirt, but her eyes looked exactly like her always-self. "Right now, I'm a LeRoy. Someday I might change my mind and go back to Pickler. But you and me? We could be called anything. Batman and Robin. Bonnie and Clyde. SpongeBob and Patrick. It would not matter what our names were. We would still be a family."

"And Dad?" asked Max.

"Dad will always be your family too. And

mine. Just in a different way. But you knew that already, didn't you?"

Max did know that. He just forgot. And remembering it made him think of something else.

By the time they got back to the Okey Doke Corral, people were folding up chairs and taking down banners.

"Let's see if we can find our hats," said Mom.

"Actually, there is something else I have to do," said Max. "Okay?"

"Okay," said Mom.

Max ran to the Family Tree table. Connie and Frank Sr. had just started rolling up the long white paper.

"Wait," said Max. He unzipped a pocket and took out a pencil. He found his name. He found Mom's name. He found a little bit of empty space near them both. In his best printing, he wrote Dad's name: *Leo LeRoy*. Then he drew a line from Dad's name to his own. He traced over the line between his name and Mom's, too, so it would be just as dark.

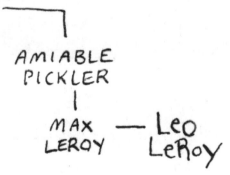

"You need to make a line between your mom and dad," said Connie, "so people will see the connection."

"I'm the connection," said Max.

"I found them!" said a voice. Max turned around. There was Mom, holding two cowboy hats. She handed one to Max. "Here you go, pardner."

Max put his hat on his head. Mom straightened it.

Mom put her hat on her head. Max straightened it. Mom laughed. *"Together We Conquer!"* she said. "Or at least, *Together We Get Our Hats on Straight.* How's that for a family motto?"

Max was not sure about the hats part. Or the

conquering part. But he was sure about the together part.

"Good," he said. Because it was.

Max and his dad love their weekends together. Weekends mean pancakes, pizza, spy games, dog walking, school projects, and surprising neighbors! Every weekend presents a small adventure as Max gets to know his dad's new neighborhood—and learns some new ways of thinking about home.

Acclaimed author Linda Urban deftly portrays a third-grader's inner world during a time of transition in this sweet and funny illustrated story that bridges the early reader and middle grade novel.

Bulletin Blue Ribbon 2016
Winner of the Center for Children's Books 2017 Gryphon Award

★ "Urban's subtle and perceptive take on divorce will resonate with children facing similar predicaments as she blends Max's worries and "someone-sitting-on-his-chest" feelings with a vivid imagination and good intentions that take father and son on some very entertaining adventures—with future ones planned."

—*Publishers Weekly,* starred review

"The cast of characters grows throughout, but at the heart of the story is Max's warm, easygoing relationship with his father."

—*Booklist*

Look for
the third book
about Max in
2019!